Ashlyn So
Illustrated by Rob Peters

Happy Snappy Wonderful Places to Go!

Happy Snappy Wonderful Places to Go
Author: Ashlyn Solinsky
Illustator: Rob Peters
Interior & Cover Layout: Michael Nicloy

ISBN: 978-1945907647

Published by
Nico 11 Publishing & Design
Mukwonago, Wisconsin
www.nico11publishing.com

Quantity order requests can be emailed to:
mike@nico11publishing.com

Printed in The United States of America

This book is dedicated to my
mom and dad, who have encouraged
me to follow my dreams, and have stood
by me every step of the way.

Thank you so much and I love you both!

I'm sitting on my swing one day,
Little Annie Rosy Rainbow,
thinking of all the things to do,
all the wonderful places to go!

Oh, the
happy
snappy
wonderful
places to go!

Hunting alligators
in the Everglades,

Skiing on mountains covered in snow!

Hiking in the desert sun,

Adventures in the great below!

Oh, the fun,
happy
snappy
wonderful
places to go!

Hunting for gold
on a pirate ship,

Riding horses
down the trail,

Sword fighting with
a swordfish king.
Are you ready
to set sail?

Oh, the
super-duper, fun,
happy snappy
wonderful
places to go!

Chicken dancing
at the royal ball,

Cliff diving in
Iceland!

Calling out the
wild beasts call,

Rock 'n' Rollin'
with the
rock band!

Oh, the beautiful,
super-duper,
fun, happy
snappy
wonderful
places to go!

Cruising the seas in a sailboat,

Riding with the Cowboys,

A great
big castle
with a giant moat,

See Santa's workshop and all the toys!

Oh, the cheery, beautiful, super-duper, fun, happy snappy wonderful places to go!

Surfing the waves
with dolphin friends,

Running through
the jungle wild!

Blasting off in
a rocket ship,

What an
adventurous child!

I'm lying in my bed one night, sleepy,
Little Annie Rosy Rainbow,

Dreaming of all these things in the world, these wonderful places to go!